$ 100

D1095925

GREAT ILLUSTRATED CLASSICS

THE PICTURE OF DORIAN GRAY

Oscar Wilde

adapted by
Fern Siegel

Illustrations by
Pablo Marcos

BARONET
B·O·O·K·S

BARONET BOOKS, New York, New York

GREAT ILLUSTRATED CLASSICS

edited by
Joshua E. Hanft

Contents

About the Author

Oscar Wilde was born in Dublin, Ireland in 1854. He was an author, playwright, and wit. He was known for preaching the importance of style in life and art and for attacking 19th-century Victorian narrow-mindedness.

At 20, Wilde left Ireland to study at Oxford University. He was an outstanding student and won a prize for his poem "Ravenna." After college, he moved to London where he became prominent in social and literary circles.

He was an early leader of the Aesthetic Movement, which believed in the concept "Art for Art's Sake." He lectured on this in England and also the United States. Wilde charmed the Americans, who were initially suspicious of this eccentric Englishman.

Oscar Wilde landed in New York. When a customs officer asked if he had anything to declare, he replied: "I have nothing to declare but my genius."

The period of his great success began in 1888 when he published *The Happy Prince*. Oscar Wilde's only novel, *The Picture of Dorian Gray,* is a moral fable.

Though he wrote books, Oscar Wilde is best known for his plays: *Lady Windermere's Fan*, *An Ideal Husband*, and *A Woman of No Importance*, all written in the late 1890s. His stage masterpiece, *The Importance of Being Earnest*, is a play noted for its epigrams (clever sayings).

In 1895, at the age of 39, Wilde was at the peak of his career. He had three hit plays running at the same time in London. That same year he brought a libel action against the Marquis of Queensbury. The trial became a social scandal and Wilde eventually lost his case. He was sentenced to two years in prison.

From his prison experiences, he wrote his best poem, *The Ballad of Reading Gaol*. On his release, Wilde left England. Ruined in health and finances, and drained of creative energy, he died in France three years later.

An Important Painting

Chapter 1

The Fateful Meeting

Basil Hallward's London studio was filled with the smell of roses. The light summer wind stirred in the trees in his garden. Through the door came the heavy scent of lilacs. Basil was a painter and he loved to surround himself with beautiful things.

He had been working on an important painting and had invited his friend, Lord Henry Wotton, to visit. Lord Henry was also a lover of beauty and, at the moment, was admiring the portrait Basil had done. The painting was of a young man about 20. His name was Dorian Gray and he was very handsome. Lord Henry was extremely impressed by his friend's talent. As the painter admired his own work, a smile of pleasure came to his rugged face.

"It is your best work, Basil, the best thing you have ever done!" Lord Henry exclaimed. "You must send it to the Academy."

As the painter looked at the gracious figure he had captured in his painting, the smile passed from his face. Then he closed his eyes and placed his fingers upon the lids, as though he was in deep thought.

After a few minutes of silent contemplation, Basil spoke. "I don't think I shall send it anywhere." He frowned, shaking his head.

"Not send it anywhere?" questioned Lord Henry. "Have you any reason? What odd chaps you painters are! You would do anything in the world to gain a reputation. But as soon as you have one, you want to throw it away. A portrait like this could make you famous," he added,

"Your Best Work!"

hoping to impress his friend.

"I know you will laugh at me, Harry, but I can't. I have put too much of myself in it," Basil said.

"But, Basil," Lord Henry laughed, raising his eyebrows and staring at him in amazement. "I can't see any resemblance. You are rugged with dark hair, this young man is blond and fair. I don't see the problem. I didn't know you were so vain, Basil. But you flatter yourself. You don't look at all like Dorian Gray."

"You don't understand me, Harry," his friend sighed. "Of course I am not like him. I should be sorry to be so. There is a destructive quality about all such physical beauty. It is better not to be so different from others."

"Basil, I was wondering. How did you meet Dorian Gray?" asked Lord Henry.

"I went to a party at Lady Brandon's. You know we poor artists have to show ourselves in society from time to time just to remind the

"I Can't See Any Resemblance!"

public we aren't savages." Basil smiled. Then he continued. "After about ten minutes I ran into Dorian Gray. It was funny but from the moment Lady Brandon introduced us, I found him to be a most fascinating person. I had a strange feeling about our meeting—I knew he would have an impact on my painting."

Basil insisted that, thanks to Dorian Gray, his recent paintings were the finest he'd ever done and stated that Dorian's personality had suggested a whole new style of art. "Yet I'm sure Dorian Gray will suffer because of his good looks."

Lord Henry was very surprised by Basil's gloomy prediction. He was eager to learn more about this mysterious young man. When he heard all this, Lord Henry wanted to meet Dorian Gray. And, although Basil was reluctant to introduce them, Lord Henry got his wish, as he was still in the studio when Basil's butler announced, "Mr. Dorian Gray to see you, sir."

"Mr. Dorian Gray to See You, Sir."

The painter suddenly looked at Lord Henry with a very serious expression on his face. "Dorian Gray has become my dearest friend, Harry," he said. "Don't try to spoil him or influence him. Your influence would be bad."

If only Lord Henry had taken his advice!

The butler showed Dorian Gray into the room. The young man immediately sat at the piano, turning over the pages of a Mozart sonata. Both Basil and Lord Henry were struck by his features. He was certainly handsome, with blue eyes and gold-colored hair. He had an aura of purity and youth that enveloped him.

But Basil worried that Lord Henry would corrupt him.

"You must lend me this sheet music, Basil. I want to learn it. It is beautiful," Dorian announced.

"That depends on how you sit for me today, Dorian," Basil replied.

"Oh, I'm tired of sitting and I don't know if I

An Aura of Purity and Youth

want a life-sized portrait of myself," Dorian answered, swinging around on the music stool in a willful manner. When he caught sight of Lord Henry, he stopped at once. "I beg your pardon, Basil, I didn't realize you had company."

"This is Lord Henry Wotton, Dorian, an old Oxford friend of mine. I have just been telling him what a terrific subject you are," Basil said.

"I have a great pleasure in meeting you, Mr. Gray," said Lord Henry, stepping forward and extending his hand. "My aunt has often spoken to me about you. You are one of her favorites."

"I am on Lady Agatha's bad list at present," replied Dorian. "I promised to go to a club in Whitechapel with her last Tuesday and I genuinely forgot all about it. We were suppose to play a duet together—three duets, I believe."

"I will make peace with my aunt. She likes you very much." Lord Henry looked at him and was again struck by his handsome features and his youth. Dorian Gray seemed curiously

"A Great Pleasure in Meeting You"

unspoiled by the world. He seemed to be good and pure.

It was at that moment that Lord Henry decided not to pay attention to Basil's warning. And, although Basil had cautioned Dorian about Lord Henry's scandalous reputation, Dorian ignored him as well.

Lord Henry's words had a profound impact on the young, impressionable Dorian. He listened excitedly as Lord Henry began to explain his theory of beauty.

"To me, beauty is the wonder of wonders. It is only shallow people who do not judge by appearances," grinned Lord Henry. He looked at the young man. "Dorian, the gods have been good to you. But what the gods give, they quickly take away. You have only a few years in which to live. Then your youth goes—and your beauty will go with it. Then you will discover that there are no more triumphs left for you."

Dorian frowned slightly at these words. But there was more to come.

Listening Excitedly!

"We Never Get Our Youth Back!"

Chapter 2

A Wish Is Granted

"Realize your youth while you still have it," Lord Henry commanded. "One day, time will catch up with you. You will become old and gray. There is such a little time that youth will last. The common hill flowers wither, but they blossom again. But we humans never get our youth back. Our limbs fail, our senses go," he said, painting a scary picture for Dorian of old age.

"We degenerate into a hideous old age, haunted by the memory of missing out on passions that frightened us and temptations we never yielded to. Don't squander your golden days. Live life! Search for new sensations! Be afraid of nothing!"

Dorian listened intently, wide-eyed and silent. Basil also heard these dangerous words and worried about the impression they would make on his inexperienced young friend. But he was too busy putting the finishing touches on Dorian's painting to warn him or to stop Sir Henry.

He stood staring at the picture for a long time, biting the end of one of his huge brushes and frowning. "It's finished," he said proudly at last. Then stooping down, he wrote his name in long red letters on the left-hand corner of the canvas.

"I congratulate you, Basil," Lord Henry said. "This is the finest portrait of any man that has been created in modern times. Dorian, come look at yourself!"

Dorian looked at the painting and blushed. The sense of his own beauty hit him like a

"It's Finished!"

lightning bolt. When he saw it, he drew back and his cheeks flushed for a moment with pleasure. A look of joy came into his eyes, as if he had seen himself for the first time.

Yet, a chill suddenly ran through him. One day he would be old and wrinkled, his slender form would be gone, and his hair would fall out.

"How awful it is," Dorian mused. "I shall grow old and horrible and dreadful. But this painting will remain always young. If it were only the other way! If only I were to be always young and the picture grew old. For that—I would give everything! I would give my soul!"

The painter stared in amazement. It was so unlike Dorian to think and speak like that. What had happened to him? Was Lord Henry's evil influence already at work?

"I am jealous of everything whose beauty does not die," said Dorian bitterly. "I know now that when one loses one's good looks, one loses everything. Your picture has taught me that.

"If Only I Were Always Young!"

Lord Henry is right. Youth is the only thing worth having. When I find that I am growing old," he cried, "I shall kill myself!"

Basil was stunned by what he heard, but before he could speak, Dorian shouted, "I am jealous of my portrait. It mocks me, Basil. I hate it! Why did you paint it?" With that, he flung himself onto the studio sofa and burst into tears.

"This is your doing, Harry," said Basil angrily.

Lord Henry shrugged his shoulders. "It is the real Dorian Gray. That is all."

Dorian barely heard Basil's charge against Lord Henry. He watched as the painter reached for a knife to rip the painting to shreds.

"Don't, Basil!" cried Dorian. "It would be murder."

"I'm glad you finally appreciate my work," the painter said coldly.

"Appreciate it? I am in love with it, Basil. It

Reaching for a Knife

is a part of myself. I feel that," Dorian explained. "I didn't mean I wished you hadn't painted it."

"As soon as it dries, it will be framed and sent to you." Basil put down the knife and spoke more gently.

Finally, Dorian calmed down. He made plans to dine with Lord Henry. Basil begged him not to go, fearing that the older man's influence would destroy his all-too-trusting friend.

But Dorian did not heed his warning. And his life would never be the same!

To Dine with Lord Henry

Grumbling Over His Newspaper

Chapter 3

A Romantic Background

At noon the next day, Lord Henry strolled from Curzon Street over to the Albany Club to call on his Uncle George. The rough-mannered old bachelor had been in the diplomatic service, but was now retired. This elderly gentleman was a hero to his butler and a terror to most of his relatives. Still, Lord Henry enjoyed his company.

When Lord Henry entered the Albany Club, he found his uncle sitting in a brown hunting jacket, smoking a cigar and grumbling over the newspaper.

"Well, Harry," said the old man, "what brings you here?"

"Family affection, Uncle George. Also, I wanted to ask you something. What I want is information about a Mr. Dorian Gray," Lord Henry replied.

"Mr. Dorian Gray? Who is he?" asked Uncle George, knitting his bushy white eyebrows.

"That's what I've come to learn. Or rather, I know who he is. He is the last Lord Kelso's grandson. His mother was Lady Margaret Devereux. I want you to tell me about his mother. What was she like? Who did she marry?"

"Kelso's grandson!" echoed the old gentleman. "Of course, I knew his mother well. She was an extraordinarily beautiful girl and made all the men frantic by running away with a penniless young fellow, a corporal in the Army.

"The poor chap was killed in a duel a few months after the marriage. There was an ugly story about it. They say Kelso paid some Belgian brute to insult his son-in-law in public,

Killed in a Duel

and then shoot him afterwards in a duel. He was a crack shot. The young man never stood a chance."

"And what happened to his wife, Dorian's mother?" asked Lord Henry.

"He brought his daughter back with him and, I am told, she never spoke to him again. The girl died, too, died within a year. She left a son." Uncle George went on to explain that Dorian's grandfather, Lord Kelso and his mother had a great deal of money. And, that by law, Dorian would inherit the family estate, Selby. "Dorian Gray," he said, "will one day be a very wealthy man."

"Thanks for the information. I always like to know everything about my new friends," smiled Lord Henry.

After exchanging pleasantries, Uncle George asked his nephew where he was lunching. "At Aunt Agatha's, both myself and Mr. Gray. He is her latest protege."

Uncle George growled approvingly and rang

"Dorian Gray Will Be a Wealthy Man."

the bell for his servant. He bid his nephew goodbye. Lord Henry walked into Burlington Street and turned his steps in the direction of Berkeley Square.

So that was the story of Dorian Gray's parents! Lord Henry was stirred by the romance and tragedy. A beautiful woman had risked everything for a mad passion! A few wild weeks of happiness cut short by a treacherous crime! The poor woman endured months of agony and then her child was born.

She was snatched away by death, the boy left alone and to the tyranny of an old and loveless man. Yes, thought Lord Henry, it was an interesting background. Dorian Gray was the son of love and death.

Stirred by Romance and Tragedy

Patiently Waiting

Chapter 4

Dorian Gray Falls in Love

One month later, Dorian Gray was sitting in an antique chair in the library of Lord Henry's house in Mayfair, a wealthy section of London. It was the charming room of an educated gentleman.

Lord Henry had placed yellow tulips in large blue china jars and on the mantelpiece. Solid oak bookcases sat against the walls. Through the small leaded panes of the window streamed the apricot-colored light of a summer's day in the city.

Dorian was patiently waiting for his friend

to return. Lord Henry had a habit of keeping people waiting. He claimed he was always late on principle. He liked to say that punctuality was the thief of time. It was another one of his sayings that meant to show how different he was from most people.

"Sorry I'm late, Dorian. I was looking for a piece of old fabric in Wardour Street and had to bargain for hours. These days people know the price of everything and the value of nothing," Lord Henry sighed.

"Your wife stopped by while I was here," Dorian told him. Lord Henry and his wife, a rather flighty, over-dressed woman, led very separate lives. Lord Henry's contempt for marriage was well-known.

"Never marry a woman with blonde hair," stated Lord Henry firmly.

"Why, Harry?" asked Dorian.

"Because they are so sentimental," he answered, adjusting his tie. "My advice to you is never marry at all."

"Never Marry at All"

"Don't worry," Dorian laughed. "I won't marry. I'm too much in love. That is one of your sayings, Harry," he blushed, "and I am putting it into practice. Her name is Sibyl Vane and she is an actress and a genius."

"Tell me about your genius," Lord Henry prodded. "How long have you known her?"

Dorian was very excited. He said that Lord Henry was responsible for his happiness, that his eccentric friend had filled him with a desire to know life. So Dorian searched all over London for new experiences.

He went everywhere—to fashionable museums and grimy back streets—looking for adventure. From St. James Park to Piccadilly Circus, Dorian sought new sensations. "I felt this London of ours must have something in store for me," he said, "with all its sinners and its sins.

"I remember that first evening we had dinner, Harry. You said the search for beauty was the real secret of life. So I took your advice and

Looking for Adventure

went searching for beauty.

"This is what happened," explained Dorian happily. "I was passing a funny little theater with great flaring gasjets and ugly playbills. A strange man stood outside it, wearing an amazing waistcoat and smoking a cigar.

"He led me to a small private box where I could watch the stage in peace. It was a third-rate curtain, colored in cupids and flowers. Women were selling oranges and ginger-beer and nuts," he added.

Dorian went on and on, describing *Romeo and Juliet*, the Shakespearean drama he watched, and how badly the orchestra played. Then, he said, he saw a beautiful young actress take the stage and, in an instance, he found passion and romance. Her voice was wonderful and her beauty unmatched. He had fallen in love immediately with actress Sibyl Vane.

"I am not surprised, Dorian, but is this the great romance of your life?" Lord Henry wondered. "You will always be loved and you will

A Young Actress

always be in love. A grand passion is the privilege of people who have nothing to do," he said, his eyes twinkling. "Still, I am curious. How did you meet her?"

"It happened the third night I went to the theater," replied Dorian. "I ran into that man again. He turned out to be Sibyl's manager. He had some connection with the theater, but insisted that the critics hated him. I had thrown Sibyl flowers one night and she had looked up at me. The old man noticed and decided to introduce me to her. I'm so glad he did!"

"What is your actress like?" asked Lord Henry.

"She is seventeen years old, with dark-brown hair, violet eyes and sweet lips. She is the prettiest thing I have ever seen in my whole life!" exclaimed Dorian. "She means everything to me. Every night I go to see her act and every night she seems to me better than the night before.

"She is so shy and gentle. Sibyl flatters me

"She Looked Up at Me!"

and says I am like a prince. Since she doesn't know my real name," he added, "she calls me Prince Charming."

Lord Henry watched his friend in amazement. How different he was from the quiet boy he had first met in Basil's studio! Dorian was growing up. He had matured and was enjoying his first love affair.

"I want you and Basil to come see Sibyl act," Dorian insisted, his eyes sparkling. "Once you see her perform, you'll appreciate her talent. I intend to rent a proper West End theater and introduce her to all the important critics. I will make my beloved Sibyl a star."

Lord Henry paused to take in Dorian's story. "Let me see. Today is Tuesday, let's meet tomorrow at the Bristol at eight o'clock. I'll bring Basil with me."

"Not eight, Harry. Let's meet at six. We must be at the theater before the curtain rises. Now I must go. Goodbye for now."

As he listened to Dorian's words, Lord Henry

"She Calls Me Prince Charming."

was conscious—and the thought brought a gleam to his brown eyes—that it was through certain words of his that Dorian Gray had fallen in love with this girl. To a large extent, he had encouraged Dorian's romantic nature. Sometimes books have a great influence. Sometimes it is a person. Lord Henry realized that he had had a great influence on the character and charm of Dorian Gray.

But who was this mystery woman who had captured Dorian's heart? Intrigued by Sibyl Vane, Lord Henry longed to meet her. The two friends parted, after agreeing to watch Sibyl perform the following night.

Later, Lord Henry sat by himself, thinking about Dorian's new-found passion. He marveled at the mysteries of love and attraction as he glanced at the scene outside his window. The sun was setting and the rooftops of the city glowed like plates of hot metal. The sky above was like a faded rose.

Lord Henry wondered what life had in store

The Two Friends Parted.

for his friend. But before he could speculate any more on the future, he got a surprise. It was a telegram from Dorian. It announced that he and Sibyl Vane were engaged to be married!

A Surprising Telegram

"Mother, I Am So Happy!"

Chapter 5

The Vane Family
Learns of the Affair

Sibyl's family was stunned by the engagement and eager to meet her young suitor. Her
mother was initially upset. She had dreamed
of Sibyl becoming a great actress. Marriage
was not in her plans for her daughter.

"Mother, I am so happy!" whispered Sibyl,
burying her face in the lap of the faded, tired-
looking older woman. Her back was turned to
the harsh light and she was sitting in a chair
in their dingy parlor.

Mrs. Vane winced and put her thin white

hands on her daughter's head. "Happy!" she echoed. "I am only happy, Sibyl, when I see you act. You must not think of anything but your acting. Mr. Isaacs has been very good to us and we owe him money."

The girl looked up and pouted. "Money, Mother?" she cried, "what does money matter? Love is more than money!"

"What do you know of this young man? You don't even know his name! However, as I've said before, if he is rich . . ." Mrs. Vane let her suggestion hang in the air.

"Mother, how can you think about money? I can only think about love," Sibyl said, her eyes sparkling. Yes, if Sibyl made a good match, it could help further the family's position in society, thought Mrs. Vane. So she had only one question for her smitten daughter: Was the young man rich? Sibyl, who sang the praises of her fiance, Prince Charming, assured her mother that he was a fine young gentleman, both wealthy and wonderful.

Was the Young Man Rich?

At that moment, the door opened and a young lad with rough brown hair came into the room. James Vane, Sibyl's brother, was stocky. His hands and feet were large and somewhat clumsy in movement. He was not as finely bred as his sister.

Nor was James as easily impressed as his greedy mother. He was very attached to Sibyl. He feared that her fiance, a rich and carefree fellow, was just playing with her affections. Why would such a man, who could keep company with a well-bred society lady, he wondered, marry a woman from the lower classes?

James Vane looked into his sister's face with tenderness. "I want you to come for a walk with me, Sibyl. I'm off to Australia tomorrow and I don't suppose I shall ever see this horrid London again."

"I'll change my clothes and meet you in a few minutes," Sibyl replied as she mounted the stairs.

"Oh, James," cried his exasperated mother,

Very Attached to Sibyl

"I wish you would stay here and get a job as a clerk in an office. Lawyers are a very respectable class, and in the country often dine with the best families. It pains me that you are leaving for Australia. I don't think there is any kind of society in the colonies."

"I hate offices and I hate clerks," he replied. "I have chosen my own life. All I ask is that you watch over Sibyl. Don't let her come to any harm. Mother, you must protect her."

"James, you talk so strangely. Of course, I will watch over our Sibyl."

"I hear a gentleman comes every night to the theater and goes backstage to talk to her. What about that?"

Mrs. Vane quickly explained to James that she had no doubt the young man was a perfect gentleman. "He is always most polite to me," she said, "and he looks rich and cultured."

"You don't know his name, though," said James harshly.

"No," admitted his mother with a placid ex-

"Watch Over Our Sibyl"

pression on her face. "He has not yet revealed his real name. He is probably a member of the aristocracy. And if he is wealthy, there is no reason," slyly suggested Mrs. Vane, "why Sibyl should not marry him."

James Vane bit his lip. "Watch over Sibyl, mother," he said again, "please watch over her."

"My son, you distress me very much. Sibyl is always under my special care. If this man is a gentleman and wealthy, there is no reason why she should not wed. He has the appearance of an aristocrat.

"I must say, it would be a brilliant marriage for Sibyl. They would make a charming couple. His good looks are really quite remarkable. Everybody notices them."

James muttered something to himself and drummed on the window with his fingers. He had just turned around to speak when the door opened and Sibyl ran in.

"How serious you both are!" she cried. "What

"How Serious You Both Are!"

is the matter?"

"Nothing," James muttered, "I suppose one must be serious sometimes. Goodbye, mother. I will have my dinner at five o'clock. Everything is packed."

"Come, Sibyl," added her brother, "let's go for our walk now." They went out into the flickering, wind-blown sunlight and strolled down the dreary Euston Road. The people passing by glanced at the unusual couple—a sullen, heavy youth and a graceful, refined-looking girl. James was like a gardener walking with a rose.

Sibyl, however, was quite unaware of the effect she was producing. She was smiling, thinking of her Prince Charming and how much she longed to see him again. Her brother James was also thinking about her suitor.

"You have a new friend, I hear. Who is he? Why have you not told me about him? He means you no good," snarled James.

"Stop, Jim!" she exclaimed. "You must not

"He Means You No Good!"

speak against him. I love him!"

"Why, you don't even know his name!" answered her brother. "Who is he? I have a right to know!"

"He is called Prince Charming. Don't you like the name? If you only saw him," said Sibyl, "you would think him the most wonderful person in the world. When you come back from Australia you will meet him. I wish you were coming to the theater tonight. He is going to be there."

"I want you to beware of him," warned James. He insistently expressed his concern for Sibyl's happiness. "If your Prince Charming ever hurts you," he growled, "I swear I will kill him!"

"I Swear I Will Kill Him!"

"Dorian Gray is Engaged to be Married!"

Chapter 6

Lord Henry and Basil
Discuss the Engagement

"I suppose you have heard the news, Basil?" asked Lord Henry that evening. Basil was being shown into the private room at the Bristol where they were having dinner.

"No, Harry," answered the artist, giving his hat and coat to the bowing waiter. "What is it?"

"Dorian Gray is engaged to be married," said Lord Henry, watching his friend carefully as he spoke.

Basil started and then frowned. "Dorian engaged to be married! It is impossible!"

"It is true," said Lord Henry.

"To whom?" Basil wanted to know at once.

"To some unknown actress," he replied.

"I can't believe it!" said Basil. "Dorian is far too sensible."

"Dorian is far too wise not to do foolish things now and again, Basil," Sir Henry proclaimed.

"Marriage is hardly a thing one can do now and again," Basil reminded his friend.

"But I didn't say he was getting married. I said he was engaged. There is a difference," smiled Lord Henry in his peculiar way.

"But think of Dorian's birth and position and wealth!" declared Basil. "It would be absurd for him to marry a girl who wasn't from his class."

"If you want to make him marry this girl, tell him that, Basil. He is sure to do it then," Lord Henry admonished.

"I hope the girl is good, Harry," sighed Basil.

"She is better than good—she is beautiful,"

"To Marry a Girl Not from His Class"

murmured Lord Henry, sipping a glass of wine.

"She may be very beautiful, Harry, but I still don't want to see Dorian tied to a bad woman," Basil stated firmly.

"You will see for yourself tonight. We are to see her at the theater. Dorian is joining us here and then taking us to meet her."

"But do you approve of it, Harry?" asked the painter, walking up and down the room and biting his lip. "It is probably just some silly childish infatuation."

"I never disapprove or approve of anything now," Lord Henry noted. "It is Dorian's decision."

Just then, Dorian himself entered. He threw off his evening cape and shook hands with both his friends.

"Harry, Basil, you both must congratulate me. I have never been so happy." Dorian was flushed with excitement and pleasure and he looked very handsome.

Flushed With Excitement

"I hope you will always be very happy, Dorian," said Basil. "How did you decide to propose to the young lady so quickly?"

Dorian told the two men that it had happened the previous night. "After I left you yesterday, Harry, I dressed, ate dinner at an Italian restaurant in Rupert Street and went to the theater. Sibyl was performing that night and was wonderful. She is a born artist. I sat in the dingy box, enthralled. I forgot that I was in London in the nineteenth century.

"When the performance was over, I went behind and spoke to her. As we were sitting together, there came a look into her eyes. My lips moved towards hers. We kissed. She trembled. It was the most perfect moment of my life," Dorian said quietly.

"Of course, our engagement is a deep secret. I don't know what my guardians will say. All I know," he said, "is that I love Sibyl Vane and I want the world to know she is mine.

"And there is something else, Harry. When

"We Kissed!"

I am with Sibyl I regret what you have taught me. I become a different man with her. The man who could wrong her would be a beast, a beast without a heart. She makes me good. When we are together, I forget all your evil, poisonous ideas," Dorian declared.

"And those are...?" asked Lord Henry, helping himself to some dessert.

"All your theories about life," Dorian replied. With that, the men ended their discussion. They finished dinner and put on their coats. A doorman hailed a carriage to take them to the theater.

Hailing a Carriage

A Fat Manager

Chapter 7

A Great Disappointment

Lord Henry and Basil were more anxious than ever to meet Sibyl Vane as they rode with Dorian in the elegant carriage to the run-down theater.

The two men were curious about the young beauty who had captured Dorian's heart. Would they be as infatuated with her as he was? Or was Dorian throwing away his chance to find a more suitable wife?

A fat manager with jeweled hands escorted them to their seats. Suddenly, amidst a round of applause, Sibyl Vane stepped onto the

79

cramped stage. Yes, she was certainly lovely to look at, Lord Henry thought, one of the loveliest women he had ever seen. The scene was from *Romeo and Juliet* and all the shabbily-dressed actors were on stage. Then, Sibyl Vane appeared. Her body swayed while she danced. Her hands seemed to be made of cool ivory.

The three men watched her perform a famous scene from the play. It was a very dramatic, moving moment, one Sibyl had done many times. Each time, she had captivated her adoring audience. But tonight, for some strange reason, Sibyl seemed dull and listless. She showed no signs of joy when, as Juliet, her eyes rested on Romeo. Her words were spoken in an artificial manner.

She acted very badly and Dorian Gray grew pale as he watched her. Basil and Lord Henry just dismissed her performance as of someone inexperienced. True, she looked charming, but her acting was terrible. When the second act was over, there came a storm of hisses.

She Acted Very Badly.

Lord Henry got up from his chair and put on his coat. "She is quite beautiful, Dorian, but she cannot act. Let us go."

Sibyl's failure to impress the audience troubled Dorian deeply. He felt humiliated in front of his best friends. "I'm sorry you both had to waste an evening," he apologized. "She is a commonplace, mediocre actress."

"Don't talk like that about anyone you love, Dorian," Basil cautioned. "I should think Miss Vane was ill. Love is more important than art."

"Don't worry about it, Dorian," advised Lord Henry. "I don't suppose you will want your wife to act after you are married so what does it matter? Come to the club with Basil and me and we will toast to the beauty of Sibyl Vane."

But Dorian could not be consoled by his friends and he asked them to leave. "Go away!" he cried. "My heart has been broken."

He sat through the remainder of the show, then rushed to Sibyl's dressing room. The girl stood there with a look of triumph on her face.

Humiliated in Front of His Friends

Her eyes were lit with fire. There was a radiance about her.

"How badly I acted tonight!" she cried.

"Horribly," he answered. "It was a dreadful performance. Are you ill?"

"I shall never act well again," she mused. "You don't understand, do you? Before I knew you acting was the only reality in my life. Tonight, for the first time, I saw the sham, the silliness of the theater.

"You gave me something better. You made me understand what love is. You are more to me than any play could ever be! My love! My Prince Charming! You mean everything to me!"

"But don't you realize what you have done? You have killed my love for you," Dorian coolly replied. He looked at her harshly.

"I loved you because you were great. Because you had such talent. Instead, I find you are shallow and stupid. What a fool I was! I will never see you again!" he screamed in anger.

"You Have Killed My Love."

Sibyl became frightened. How could her Prince Charming be so mean to her? He had said he loved her, he had kissed her and promised her the world. Why had he changed so? Sibyl started to cry and, as she fell to the floor, she grabbed Dorian's knees, clutching at him for dear life.

"Please don't be cruel to me, dearest. I will work hard and try to improve myself. I promise you I will be a better actress next time. I love you so much. Please don't leave me," she begged.

Dorian looked down at her with angry eyes. His upper lip curled in disdain. He became hard and brutal. Her tears did not melt his icy heart. He flung Sibyl aside and turned on his heel.

"I'm going," he said in a calm, clear voice. "I can't see you any more. You have bitterly disappointed me." With that, he stormed out of the theater.

Hard and Brutal

The Face Had Changed.

Chapter 8

The Horror Begins

Dorian wandered around Covent Garden for hours that night, upset and confused. Huge carts filled with flowers rumbled slowly down empty streets. He watched the farmers unload their wagons. All the while, he was racked by pain and disappointment. In the morning, tired and exhausted, he returned to his mansion.

As he opened the door, his eyes fell on the portrait Basil Hallward had painted of him. He was startled by what he saw. The face appeared to have changed! Was such a thing possible? It was strange, but the expression *was* different—there was a touch of cruelty in the mouth that had not been there before.

Could he be dreaming? Dorian examined the painting more closely. He opened the blinds. The bright dawn light flooded the room. The strange expression on the painting remained. He picked up a mirror and examined his own face. His features were the same—only the mouth of the painting was distorted.

He wasn't dreaming. It was horrible! What did it mean? He threw himself into a chair to think. Suddenly, he remembered the words he had spoken in Basil's studio the day the painting was finished.

He had made a crazy wish: He asked to remain young and for the portrait to grow old. Now, his mad desire had come true. Dorian's face would remain young and handsome and the canvas would bear the burden of his sins!

But such things were impossible. It seemed monstrous to even think of them. And yet, there was the picture before him—with that

Picking Up a Mirror

definite touch of cruelty in the mouth.

Dorian, a selfish man, thought only of his own destiny. He did not think about the pain he had caused Sibyl Vane. Instead, he reserved his pity for a great work of art. He was saddened that its beauty had changed.

He suddenly realized that this scary painting held the secrets of his life! It told his story. It had changed already. Its gold would wither into gray. Its color and fire would die. It was terrible! For every sin that he committed, his portrait would pay the price. What had he done? Would a painting teach him to hate his own soul?

Frightened by this mystery, Dorian resolved never to sin again. He would resist temptation. He would not see Lord Henry any more, not listen to his poisonous theories.

Dorian decided that he would go back to Sibyl Vane, make his apologies and marry her. He realized that he had been selfish and cruel to Sibyl. But he would make it up to her. They

His Portrait Would Pay the Price.

would be happy and their life together would be beautiful and pure.

Dorian Gray got up from his chair and drew a large screen right in front of the portrait, shuddering as he glanced at it. He walked to the door and opened it. When he stepped out on the grass, he grew a deep breath. The fresh morning air seemed to drive away all his demons. His thoughts were only of Sibyl when he went to bed at last.

The Fresh Morning Air

Looking Over His Letters

Chapter 9

A Rude Awakening

It was long past noon when he awoke. Victor, his French valet, had crept several times on tiptoe into the room to see if he was stirring. Finally, his bell sounded, and Victor came in quietly with a cup of tea and a pile of letters.

After a few minutes, Dorian got up, threw on a cashmere bathrobe and went into the bathroom. The cool water refreshed him and he seemed to forget the argument of the previous night. He returned to his bedroom, sipped some weak tea, and looked over his letters.

One was from Lord Henry, and had been

brought by messenger that morning. He hesitated, then put it aside. The others he opened. They contained the usual assortment of invitations to dinner, tickets to private art showings and programs for charity concerts.

Suddenly, his eye fell on the screen that he had placed in front of the portrait. Was it all true? Had the portrait really changed? Or had it simply been his over-active imagination that had made him see a look of evil where there had been a look of joy? Surely a painting could not change.

He knew that when he was alone, he would have to examine the portait. When the coffee had been brought, Victor left the room. Then Dorian rose from the bed and threw himself down on a Spanish couch that stood facing the screen.

What if by some fate or deadly chance someone else should see the horrible changes? What would he do if Basil wanted to see his picture again? Dorian got up and locked both

Had the Portrait Really Changed?

doors. At least he would be alone when he looked upon his mask of shame. Then he drew the screen aside and saw himself face to face. It was perfectly true. The portrait had changed!

It was incredible! How could such a thing occur? Was there some connection between the picture painted on the canvas and the soul that was within him? He gazed at the picture in sickened horror and fear.

Dorian realized that one thing the changed portrait had done was to make him see how unjust, how cruel he had been to Sibyl Vane. It was not too late to make amends. She could still be his wife. His selfishness would be transformed into some nobler passion.

Finally, he decided to write a letter to Sibyl, to beg her forgiveness, to say how much he loved her. As he finished his letter, there was a knock at the door. His servant announced that Lord Henry was anxious to see him. Without waiting for permission, Lord Henry rushed

Horror and Fear

into Dorian's bedroom.

"I'm so sorry, Dorian," Lord Henry began.

"Do you mean about Sibyl Vane?" Dorian asked.

"Did you go see her after the play?" his friend inquired.

"Yes, and I was brutal to her," admitted Dorian. "But I'm better now. I have decided that from now on I will be good. I want to marry Sibyl. I'm going to go see her today and ask her to forgive me for my terrible behavior."

"It's too late!" cried Lord Henry. "Sibyl Vane is dead!"

A cry of pain broke from the Dorian's lips and he leaped to his feet. "Dead! Sibyl dead! It is not true! It is a horrible lie! How dare you say it?"

"It is quite true, Dorian," said Lord Henry gravely. "It is in all the morning papers. I wrote to you this morning to ask you not to see anyone until I came. There will be an inquest of course, and you must not be mixed up in it.

A Cry of Pain

There would be a terrible scandal if you were. Do they know your name at the theater?" he asked. "If they don't, it's all right. Did anyone see you going to her dressing room last night? That is important."

Dorian did not answer for a few moments. He was dazed with horror. Finally, he stammered, in a stifled voice, "Harry, I can't bear it! Please tell me everything that happened."

"I Can't Bear It!"

Lying Dead on the Floor

Chapter 10

Sibyl Commits Suicide

Lord Henry explained that as Sibyl was leaving the theater with her mother, she claimed to have forgotten something in her dressing room. When she didn't come back down, the stage manager went to get her. He found her lying dead on the floor. She had swallowed some poison and died instantly.

"I have murdered Sibyl Vane," Dorian said, hanging his head in shame, "murdered her as surely as if I had cut her little throat with a knife."

Lord Henry consoled his friend, insisting

that Sibyl was an overly-romantic girl who had taken her own life. No one was to blame, he said.

Dorian listened to Lord Henry's words. He felt the time had come to make up his own mind.

Or had the choice already been made? Life itself had decided for him. Eternal youth, passion, wild joys and wilder sins—these things would be his.

"Oh, Harry, how I loved her once! It seems years ago to me now. She was everything to me. Then came that dreadful night—was it really only last night—when she acted so badly, and my heart broke.

"She explained it all to me. But I wasn't moved a bit. I thought Sibyl was shallow. Then something happened that made me afraid. I can't tell you what it was," he said, thinking about the strange painting. "But it decided for me. I would go back to Sibyl."

Lord Henry listened to his friend without

Consoling Words

speaking. He found the suicide a dramatic interlude at best; in truth, he cared only for Dorian's reputation.

"Harry," cried Dorian Gray, coming over and sitting beside him, "I don't feel this tragedy. Am I heartless?"

"No, you are only very young and very romantic. In time, you will recover. Come with me to the opera tonight, it will help you to forget," Lord Henry counseled.

Dorian quickly accepted the invitation. He vowed not to think about Sibyl again. To Dorian, his own happiness would be all that mattered. He would quickly forget about the dead Sibyl Vane.

"You have helped me through a bad time, Harry. I wonder what life has in store for me now," he said.

"Life has everything in store for you, Dorian. There is nothing that you, with your extraordinary good looks, your charm, and your resources, will not be able to do."

The Opera Tonight

Strong words, yet a feeling of pain crept over Dorian as he thought of the desecration in store for his portrait. Now it would become a monster! The shame of it all would have to be hidden away!

For a moment he thought of praying that the horrible connection that existed between him and the picture might end. It had changed in answer to a prayer. Perhaps a new prayer might undo the old one.

But Dorian did not pray. He could not give up the chance to remain forever young. This portrait would be the most magical of mirrors.

If only he hadn't been so foolish and so vain! His life would never be the same!

Desecration of His Portrait

Offering Sympathy

Chapter 11

Basil Almost Discovers
the Dreaded Secret

The next day Basil Hallward came by to see Dorian. He wanted to offer his sympathy about Sibyl's death. He also wanted to ask his friend if he would let him exhibit his portrait in a Paris gallery.

Dorian was eating lunch when Basil was shown into the room. "I read of Sibyl in the late edition of *The Globe* I picked up at my club. I came here at once," said Basil. "I can't tell you how sorry I am. I know you must feel terrible. Did you go down and see the girl's mother?"

"Of course not," murmured Dorian Gray, as he sipped yellow wine from a Venetian glass and looked bored. "I was at the opera."

"You went to the opera!" exclaimed Basil, shocked at Dorian's callous behavior. "You went to the opera while Sibyl Vane lay dead?"

"Stop talking about it!" cried Dorian. "What is past is past."

"You call yesterday the past?" asked his horrified friend. "Dorian, this is horrible. Something has changed you completely. You talk as if you had no heart, no pity. It is all Harry's bad influence."

Dorian brushed away Basil's words with a wave of his hand. "I don't want to be at the mercy of my emotions. A man who is master of himself can end a sorrow as easily as he can invent a pleasure. I want you to draw me a picture of Sibyl, Basil. I should like to have something to remember her by."

"All right," Basil agreed, "if it would please

"Something Has Changed You!"

you. But you must then do something for me. Please come to my studio and sit for another portrait."

"I can never sit for you again, Basil. It is impossible!" Dorian swore angrily.

The painter stared at him. "Don't be ridiculous. Don't you like the painting I did of you?" Basil asked. "Why have you pulled the screen in front of it? It is the best picture I have ever done. It is disgraceful of you to hide my work away."

"The light was too strong on the portrait," Dorian hastily explained.

"Too strong! Surely not. It's a great place to hang it. Let me see it." Basil walked towards the corner of the room.

A cry of terror broke from Dorian Gray's lips and he rushed between the painter and the screen. "You must not look at it!"

"Why shouldn't I look at it?" asked Basil, laughing.

"If you try to look at it, Basil, on my word of

"You Must Not Look at It!"

honor, I will never speak to you again. I'm very serious."

Basil was thunderstruck and he looked at Dorian in absolute amazement. He had never seen him like this before. Dorian was actually pale with rage. His hands were clenched and he was shaking all over.

"I won't look at it if you don't want me to," he said coldly, turning on his heel and going over towards the window. "But really, it's strange I'm not allowed to see my own work, especially as I am going to exhibit it in Paris in the fall."

"To exhibit it! You want to exhibit it?" exclaimed Dorian, a great sense of fear creeping over him. Was the world going to be shown his secret?

"Why should you object?" asked Basil. "If you keep it behind a screen, you must not like it very much."

Dorian Gray passed his hand over his forehead. There were beads of sweat there. He felt

Pale with Rage

that he was on the brink of a terrible danger. "You can't have forgotten that you assured me that you wouldn't exibit the painting," cried Dorian. Then he remembered that Lord Henry had said to him once, half jokingly, that he should ask Basil why he would not exhibit Dorian's portrait before.

"Basil," he said, looking his friend in the eye. "What was your reason for refusing to exhibit my picture before now?"

The painter shuddered in spite of himself. "Dorian, if I told you, you would laugh at me. If you don't want me to see your picture, I won't ask again. Your friendship is more important to me than the painting."

"No, Basil, you must tell me," insisted Dorian. "I have a right to know." He was determined to find out Basil Hallward's mystery.

"Sit down, Dorian," said the painter, looking troubled. "And just answer me one question: Have you noticed something curious in the painting? Something that didn't strike you at

"Sit Down, Dorian!"

first, but was later revealed to you?"

"Basil!" screamed Dorian, clutching the arms of his chair and staring at him with wild eyes.

"I see you did. Don't speak," replied Basil. "Your personality had the most extraordinary influence over me. One day—a fatal day, I think—I decided to paint a portrait of you as you are. Whether it was the realism of the method or the wonder of your personality, something happened. I worked very hard and it was a great success. But I had put too much of myself into it. My praise for you was too great. So I decided not to allow the picture to be exhibited."

Basil continued. "It is amazing to me, Dorian, that you should have seen this in the portrait."

"I saw something," the young man answered slowly, "something that seemed curious."

"Well, then, " said Basil relieved, "you won't mind now if I exhibit the work."

"Basil!"

"Never," growled Dorian.

Basil decided not to argue with his friend and agreed to his odd request. "It's your decision and I respect it, Dorian. Goodbye for now. You have been the one person in my life who has really influenced my art."

Basil picked up his hat and coat and turned to his friend. "You will sit for me again?" he asked.

"Impossible!" Dorian said. "I can't explain it to you, Basil, but I must never sit for you again. There is something fatal about a portait. It has a life of its own."

He bid Basil goodbye and closed the door. Suddenly, Dorian Gray smiled to himself. He had succeeded in fooling his friend. Basil would never learn the truth about the awful portait. Still, he grew worried. The portrait must be hidden away at all costs. He could not run such a risk of discovery again!

"It Has a Life of Its Own."

Hiding His Tortured Painting

Chapter 12

An Evil Book
Changes Everything

The day after Sibyl's suicide, Dorian decided to hide his tortured painting. What if someone else saw it? What would they think? He ordered his servant to take the painting to the third floor of his townhouse and store it in his old playroom.

His trusted servant was given strict orders. No one was allowed to enter the room. Only Dorian had the key to unlock its thick wooden door. There, he thought, his dreadful secret would be safe from the world.

As the door closed, Dorian put the key in his pocket and looked at the room that would house his secret. His eyes fell on a large 17th-century purple satin cover his grandfather had found in a convent in Italy. Yes, that would serve to wrap the dreadful painting. It had often wrapped the dead. Now it would hide something that had a corruption of its own. Worse than the corruption of death—something that would breed horrors but would never die!

He turned, locked the door and went downstairs to his sitting room. He picked up the St. James *Gazette*. The newspaper was full of reports of Sibyl's death. Fortunately for Dorian, his name was never mentioned. Relieved that he had avoided any bad publicity, Dorian was once more determined to think only of his own pleasure in the future.

It was just after 5 o'clock when the doorbell rang. A messenger had a package from Lord Henry. To cheer Dorian up, Lord Henry had

Wrapping the Dreadful Painting

sent him a little yellow book. It was the strangest book Dorian had ever read in his life!

It chronicled all the sins of the world. The novel had no plot and only one character—a young Parisian man who spent his life trying to realize, in the nineteenth century, all the passions of every century before his own. It was a book of evil.

But Dorian was so fascinated that he could not stop reading. For years to come, Dorian Gray would never free himself from the influence of this evil book. He never even tried. Instead, he ordered no less than nine large-paper copies of the first edition from Paris.

He had them bound in different colors so they might suit his moods. The hero, a young Parisian in whom the romantic and scientific temperments blended, very much resembled Dorian Gray. The character was so much like him that this strange novel seemed to contain the story of his life—even before he had lived it!

A Strange Book

THE PICTURE OF DORIAN GRAY

The good looks that had been captured in Basil's painting of Dorian captivated others as well. Even those who heard the most evil things about Dorian Gray could not believe them. He didn't look evil at all. Instead, he had the look of someone who kept himself pure.

Yet Dorian began to live the life written about in Lord Henry's book. And it was so easy. He was rich. His handsome features captivated everyone who met him. He knew joy and cruelty. He could have whatever he wanted.

Strange tales began circulating around London about him. He still looked pure, but was he? Dorian would disappear on long, mysterious absences. Afterwards, he would creep upstairs to the locked room and stand in front of the portrait that Basil had painted.

There, he would look at the evil, ugly, aging face on the canvas. He grew more and more taken with his own looks, and more and more interested in the corruption of his own soul!

No one knew where he went. No one knew

In Front of the Portrait

about the sordid room in the nasty tavern near the docks. Traveling in disguise and under an assumed name, Dorian Gray would frequent this awful place.

All the sins he had read about in the little yellow book became real to him. With wild abandon, Dorian Gray fed his mad hunger for adventure and destruction! He indulged his every mood, every whim, every want. He mined the deep mysteries of all the senses.

At the same time, Dorian was known as a man-about-town. He was famous for dressing well. He was rich and indulged his every whim. He began to collect musical instruments, expensive jewels, and beautiful works of art. He had a house in London and a huge estate in the country.

He spent his money recklessly.

But all these treasures, everything he collected, were just a means of escape. Hanging on the walls of the lonely locked room where he had spent his childhood, he had hung the

Traveling in Disguise

terrible portrait whose constantly changing features showed him the real degradation of his life.

He had draped the purple and gold Italian curtain over it to hide it from view. For weeks he would not go to the locked room and he'd forget the hideous painted thing. For a time, he would enjoy a light-hearted and joyous existence.

Then, suddenly, at night he would creep out of the house, and go to dreadful places near Blue Gate Fields and stay—day after day—until he was driven away. On his return, he would sit in front of the picture—somtimes hating it and himself. After a few years, he could not bear to be parted from the painting for long periods of time. He gave up the villa he had shared with Lord Henry in Italy and the little white house in Algiers where they would spend the winter.

Dorian Gray worried about the painting that was now such a part of his life. What if it

The Real Degradation

was stolen? Or what if, while he was away, someone gained access to the rooom, in spite of the bars, and learned his secret! The very thought terrified him. What if the world already suspected?

After all, there were people who distrusted him. He was nearly blackballed at a West End club. Once, when he was brought by a friend into his London club, the Duke of Berwick and another gentleman got up and left!

By his 25th birthday, wild stories were again circulating in polite society. It was said that Dorian Gray had been seen fighting with foreign sailors, that he kept company with thieves and other criminals.

Women who had adored him, now shunned him. Respectable men would leave the room if he entered their club. What had happened to the once innocent boy? Only Dorian Gray knew the answer. He had been poisoned by Lord Henry's book.

To him, evil was now beautiful.

Fighting with Foreign Sailors

A Man with a Bag

Chapter 13

Basil Tries To Save His Friend

Thirteen years later, on the ninth of November, on the eve of his 38th birthday, Dorian was walking home. He had dined at Lord Henry's and the night was cold and foggy.

At the corner he passed a man with a bag in his hand. Dorian recognized Basil Hallward. A strange sense of fear, which he did not understand, came over him. He did not want to speak to Basil, so he pretended not to recognize him. Dorian walked quickly in the direction of his house.

But Basil had spotted Dorian and placed his

hand on Dorian's arm. "Dorian! I have been waiting for you in your library. I'm off to Paris by the midnight train. I'll be gone for six months. I wanted to speak to you before I left. I thought it was you. But I wasn't sure. Didn't you recognize me?"

"In this fog, Basil? Why, I can't even recognize Grosvenor Square. I'm sorry that you are going away, I haven't seen you for ages."

"Here we are," said Basil. "I really must speak to you. It is most important."

"All right. You'd better come in," said the weary Dorian.

Basil followed Dorian into the library. There was a bright wood fire blazing in the large open hearth. Brandy and soda stood on a table nearby.

"I can't wait any longer, Dorian. There is something I must say to you," Basil stated.

"What do you want to talk about, Basil?" asked Dorian. "I'm very tired and I want to go to bed."

"I Must Speak to You."

"It's about you. I think you should know that the most terrible things are being said against you in London. Your reputation is in ruins," said Basil sadly.

"I don't care what other people gossip about," replied Dorian, and he sighed. "I only care about other people's scandals."

"You must care, Dorian. Of course, I don't believe the horrible things people say. I think sin is something that writes itself across a man's face. It cannot be hidden. You look as young and pure as you did when we first met.

"Yet I see you very seldom," he continued, "and I hear such hideous things. Why do so many gentlemen refuse to go to your house or invite you to theirs? Why is your friendship so fatal to other people?" Basil ticked off a list of prominent men who had been ruined by Dorian Gray.

He mentioned a young royal son who had committed suicide in the Navy, Lord Kent's son who married a prostitute, and the scandal

"Your Reputation is in Ruins."

of Adrian Singleton, who had been convicted of forgery. All of them had once been close friends of Dorian Gray

"And that's not all," added Basil miserably. "It's said you have been seen creeping out of dreadful houses at dawn and sneaking in disguise into the foulest dens near the wharf. Can such rumors be true? Don't you care about your reputation?"

Dorian shrugged. He seemed completely indifferent to Basil's words. He acted as if he did not care about the terrible stories that were circulating.

"I wonder," mused Basil, "if I really do know you. Before I answer, I'd have to see your soul."

"My soul!" muttered Dorian Gray, jumping up from the sofa and turning almost white with fear. "Fair enough. You shall see my soul for yourself tonight. Follow me. It is your handiwork. Why shouldn't you look at it? You have chattered enough about corruption and disgrace. Now you shall see it face to face."

Creeping Out of Dreadful Houses

Basil became frightened. His friend seem so reckless. Dorian Gray sneered at Basil with contempt. "Come upstairs, Basil," he said quietly. "I keep a diary of my life. See for yourself."

There was a madness of pride in every word Dorian spoke. He stamped his foot on the ground in a boyish manner. He felt a terrible joy at someone else sharing his secret. The man who had painted the portrait was about to be burdened for the rest of his life with the hideous memory of what he had done!

"Come Upstairs, Basil!"

The Locked Studio

Chapter 14

The Truth Is Revealed

They walked silently up to the locked studio. The lamp cast fantastic shadows on the wall and staircase. A rising wind made the windows rattle.

"You insist on knowing, Basil?" Dorian asked in a low voice.

"Yes," he replied with certainty.

"Shut the door behind you," Dorian commanded. "You are the one man in the world who is entitled to know everything about me. You have had more to do with my life than you think."

Basil glanced around the room with a puzzled expression. It looked as if it had not been lived in for years. A faded tapestry, a curtained picture, an almost empty bookcase, a table and chair—that was all it contained. As Dorian was lighting a half-burned candle, he saw the whole place was covered with dust and the carpet was full of holes.

"So you think it is only God who sees the soul, Basil? Draw that curtain back, and you will see mine!" he said in a voice that was cold and cruel.

"You are sounding crazy, Dorian," Basil said, seized by a sudden fear.

"I will do it myself," said the angry young man. He tore the curtain from its rod and flung it to the ground. An exclamation of terror broke from Basil's lips.

He saw in the dim light a hideous face on the canvas. It grinned wickedly at him! Something in the expression filled him with disgust and hatred. Good heavens! It was Dorian

Grinning Wickedly at Him

Gray's own face. The horror had not entirely spoiled the beauty. There was still some gold in the thinning hair and some red on the handsome mouth. The sunken eyes were still blue. Yes, it was Dorian Gray. But who had done it?

He seemed to recognize his own brushwork; the frame was his design. The idea was monstrous, and he was gripped by fear. He seized the lighted candle and held it to the picture. In the left-hand corner was his own name, traced in long letters of bright red.

His own picture! What did it mean? Why had it changed? And how had it done so?

"What does this mean?" cried Basil, frightened by what he had seen. He turned and looked at Dorian Gray with the eyes of a sick man. His mouth and hands twitched and he was unable to speak. He passed his hand across his forehead. It was covered in sweat.

Dorian spoke. "Years ago, when I was a boy, you painted a portrait of me. You flattered me and taught me to be vain about my looks. One

"What Does This Mean?"

day you introduced me to Lord Henry, who told me the only thing of value was beauty.

"Your portrait of me made me think I was handsome," said Dorian, as he clenched his fist. "I didn't want to lose my good looks. In a mad moment, I made a wish. Perhaps you remember it?"

"I remember it! But it is impossible."

"What is impossible?" murmured Dorian, pointing to the horrifying painting. "This is my soul."

"You once told me you had destroyed my painting," said Basil.

"I was wrong," said Dorian. "It has destroyed me."

"You were such an ideal to me," Basil said, shaking his head in wonder. "This hideous painting has the eyes of a devil! If it is true, if this is what you have done with your life, you must be worse than people say." Basil shuddered. "The horror in the painting is from within. That is from where the foulness has come."

"This Is My Soul!"

"Let Us Pray Together!"

Chapter 15

A Murder Is Committed

Basil flung himself into the rickety chair that was standing by the table and buried his face in his hands. Dorian was sobbing at the window.

"What a lesson, Dorian! What an awful lesson! Pray, Dorian, pray," instructed Basil. "What are we taught in boyhood? 'Forgive us our sin.' Let us pray together. The prayer of your pride was answered. The prayer of your repentance will also be answered. I admired your beauty too much—we are both punished."

"It is too late, Basil," Dorian faltered.

"It is never too late, Dorian. Let us kneel down. You have done enough evil in your life. Don't you see that accursed painting leering at us?"

Dorian Gray glanced at the picture and suddenly felt an uncontrollable feeling of hatred for Basil Hallward. The mad passions of a cornered animal stirred within him. He hated the man seated at the table more than he had ever hated anything in his whole life.

He glanced wildly around. His eye fell on a knife that was lying on the top of a chest. He moved slowly towards it, passing Basil.

As soon as he got behind him, he seized the knife. Dorian quietly turned around and plunged the knife behind Basil's ear, crushing the man's head down on the table, and stabbing him again and again.

There was a stifled groan and the wretched sound of someone choking with blood. Basil's arms shot up and grabbed at the air. Dorian stabbed him twice more, as blood began drip-

He Seized the Knife.

ping to the floor. Basil did not move. Then Dorian threw the knife on the table and listened. Silence.

He could hear nothing but the dripping of blood on the threadbare carpet. He opened the door and went out on the landing. He peered over the railing into the black seething well of darkness. The house was absolutely quiet. Then he took out the key and returned to the room, locking himself in.

How quickly it had been done! Dorian Gray felt strangely calm, and walking over to the window, opened it and stepped out on the balcony. The wind had blown the fog away and the sky was like a peacock's tail, starred with rows of golden eyes.

He looked down and saw the policeman making his rounds, flashing the long beam of his lantern on the doors of the silent houses. A woman in a fluttering shawl was staggering along.

A bitter blast of wind swept across the

The Dripping of Blood

square. The gaslamps flickered and became blue, and the leafless trees shook their branches back and forth. Dorian shivered and closed the window. He felt haunted and longed to escape from this room of death and decay.

There was no time to delay. He must leave the room at once. He did not glance at the murdered man. The friend who had painted the fatal portrait had gone out of his life. That was enough.

Dorian locked the door behind him, and crept quietly downstairs. He saw Basil's coat and bag. He hid them away and began to think. What evidence was there against him? Basil had left the house at eleven. No one had seen him come in again. Most of the servants were at his country estate. Basil was scheduled to go to Paris by the midnight train. It would be months before his absence aroused suspicion. Months! All the evidence could be destroyed by then!

A sudden thought struck him—he needed

Hiding the Evidence

an alibi. He put on his coat and hat and went outside. After a few moments, he rang the bell. In five minutes his valet, looking very drowsy, answered the door.

"I'm sorry to wake you up, Francis," he said. "But I forgot my key. Did anyone call for me this evening?"

"Mr. Hallward, sir, but he left at eleven to catch his train."

"Oh! I'm sorry I missed him. Did he leave any message?" asked Dorian slyly.

"No sir, except that he would write to you from Paris."

"Thank you. That will be all, Francis. Call me at nine o'clock tomorrow morning. Good-night."

"I Forgot My Key."

Sleeping Peacefully

Chapter 16

Erasing the Crime

At nine o'clock the next morning, Dorian's servant came in with a cup of hot chocolate and opened the shutters. The man had to touch him twice on the shoulder before he woke up. Dorian was sleeping quite peacefully. He looked like a little boy who had been tired out by healthy play.

He turned around and leaning on his elbow, sipped his chocolate. The mellow November sun came streaming into the room. The sky was bright and there was a warmth in the air. It was almost like a morning in May.

But gradually, the events of the previous night crept, with blood-stained feet, into his brain. He winced at the memory of what he had done and was again seized by a hatred for Basil Hallward. He had killed a man! And the dead man was still in his house!

After he finished his drink, he sat down at the table and wrote two letters. One he put in his pocket. The other he handed to his valet and ordered him to deliver it to a Mr. Alan Campbell, 152 Hertford Street. Dorian wanted Alan Campbell to come immediately to his home.

Dorian passed the morning sketching and reading. But he was troubled by his thoughts. What if Alan Campbell was out of the country? Worse yet, what if he refused to see him? After all, they were no longer friends. They had been great friends once, five years before. Then the closeness had ended. Suddenly. Completely. Now when they met in society, it was only Dorian Gray who spoke. Alan Campbell never replied.

Writing Letters

Alan was an extremely smart young man who loved science. At Cambridge, he spent a great deal of time working in his laboratory. He was an excellent musician as well and it was music that had first brought Alan Campbell and Dorian Gray together.

Whether or not a quarrel had taken place no one ever knew. But people remarked that they scarcely spoke when they met and Campbell seem to leave any party when Dorian Gray was present. He had changed too—Alan was very depressed, began to dislike music, and absorbed himself completely in his scientific research.

Dorian began to pace the hallway. The suspense was unbearable. Time seemed to be crawling with feet of lead. At last the door opened. "Mr. Campbell, sir," said the valet. A sigh of relief broke from Dorian's lips.

"Ask him to come in at once, Francis." Dorian felt he was himself again. He would be able to destroy the evidence quickly.

Working In His Laboratory

Alan Campbell walked in, looking stern and rather pale. Campbell sat in a chair by the table and Dorian sat opposite him. The two men's eyes met. Dorian knew what he was about to do was dreadful!

"Thank you for coming, Alan."

"Your note said it was a matter of life and death," said Alan. "I don't care. I came to tell you that. I want nothing to do with you. I refuse to get mixed up in your life or your shameful secrets." Dorian listened quietly to Alan's angry words. He collected his thoughts and leaned forward, speaking softly. "Alan, I murdered a man. He had more to do with my life than you realize. Alan, I need your help in destroying the body. You are a doctor," added Dorian, "you know how to get rid of it for me. You are the one man who is able to save me. I am forced to bring you into this matter. I have no option."

"I have no desire to help you, Dorian," Alan declared.

"Alan, I Murdered a Man!"

"Alan, you are scientific-minded. You know about chemistry and things of that nature. You have made experiments. What you have got to do is destroy the body that is upstairs—destroy it so that not a trace of it will be left," Dorian instructed.

"Nobody saw this person come into the house. Indeed, at the present moment, he is supposed to be in Paris. He will not be missed for months. When he is missed, there must be no trace of him found here. You, Alan, must change him and everything that belongs to him into a handful of ashes that I can scatter into the air."

"You are mad, Dorian," replied Alan Campbell coolly. "Mad to imagine that I would raise a finger to help you after this monstrous confession. I will have nothing to do with the matter. I don't care what shame you endure. You deserve it!"

"You must have something to do with it. Wait and listen to me, Alan," insisted Dorian.

"Destroy the Body!"

"Murder! Good God, Dorian! Is that what you have come to? I won't inform the police. It's none of my business. Besides, you are certain to be arrested. Nobody ever commits a crime without doing something stupid. But I will have nothing to do with it."

Dorian listened to his former friend without expression. Then he stated, in a firm manner, "All I ask, Alan, is that you perform a certain scientific experiment. You go to the hospitals and dead-houses and the horrors there don't affect you. If in some hideous laboratory you found this man lying on a table with slashes all over his body, you would simply look at him as an interesting subject.

"You would not believe you were doing anything wrong. What I want you to do, Alan, is merely what you have done before. And remember, it is the only piece of evidence against me. If it is discovered, I am lost. And it is sure to be discovered unless you help me."

A look of pity, mixed with anger, came into

"I Will Have Nothing to Do with It!"

Dorian Gray's eyes. "Alan, I beg you," said Dorian. "Think of the position that I am in. Just before you came I was seized with terror. Please, we were friends once."

"Don't speak to me about those days. They are dead," replied Alan.

"But, Alan, if you don't help me, I'm ruined. The authorities will hang me!" Dorian shouted.

"There is no good begging, Dorian," Alan stated firmly. "I absolutely refuse to do anything in the matter. It is insane of you to ask me. If you have gotten yourself into serious trouble, it is no concern of mine. You committed the problem, you'll have to solve it."

"You are sure you refuse to help me?" Dorian asked one last time.

"I refuse," said Alan.

Dorian paused for a moment, then took a piece of paper and wrote something on it. He folded it carefully and gave it to Campbell, who read it and fell back in his chair. As he read it, his face turned ghastly pale. A horri-

Falling Back in His Chair

ble sense of sickness came over him. Alan felt as if his heart was beating itself to death!

After two or three minutes of terrible silence, Dorian spoke. "I'm sorry, Alan. But you leave me no choice. If you don't help me, I will send the letter I have written to the name on that paper. It is impossible for you to refuse me now."

Campbell nodded miserably. He buried his face in his hands and a shudder passed through him. He knew that he had no choice—if he refused Dorian Gray it meant ruin for himself!

"Yes, it is my turn to dictate terms, Alan. You know what they are. Just do what I ask." Dorian placed his hand on Alan's shoulder and the weight seemed to crush him. Admitting defeat, he asked Dorian to contact his assistant and to secure the necessary tools. Once they arrived, Dorian escorted him upstairs to the playroom.

Dorian opened the door and he saw the face

Admitting Defeat

of his portrait in the sunlight. He remembered that the night before he had forgotten, for the first time in his life, to hide the fatal canvas. How horrible it was! What was that red dew that glistened on one of the hands? Had the canvas sweated blood?

Without looking further, Dorian grabbed the torn cover and flung it over the possessed painting.

"Leave me alone," ordered Alan. "It will take several hours."

By dinner time, Alan returned downstairs. "I have done what you asked," he said bitterly. "Now I never want to see you again."

The Fatal Canvas

To Forget the Past

Chapter 17

Revenge!

A cold rain began to fall and the blurred streetlamps looked eerie in the dripping mist. The moon hung low in the sky like a yellow skull. Dorian wanted only to forget the past few hours.

Dorian Gray hailed a cab and told the driver to take him to the docks. He screamed at the man to driver faster and faster. On the way, they passed public-houses that were just closing and men and women who were clustering in broken groups around their doors. From some of the bars came sounds of horrible laughter. In others, drunks brawled and screamed.

Lying back in the hansom cab, with his hat pulled over his forehead, Dorian Gray watched with dull eyes the sordid shame of London. He repeated to himself the words that Lord Henry had said to him on that fateful day when they met in Basil's studio: "To cure the soul by means of the senses, and the senses by means of the soul." Yes, thought Dorian, that was the secret.

There were opium dens where one could buy oblivion. Yes, that was the answer. He had done it before and would do it again.

The hideous hunger for opium seized him. Suddenly, the driver drew up the horses with a jerk at the top of a dark lane. Over the low roofs and jagged chimney stacks of the houses rose the black masts of ships. A wreath of white mist clung like ghostly sails to the ship-yards.

"Somewhere about here, sir, ain't it?" the

The Sordid Shame of London

driver asked.

Dorian started and peered around. "This will do," he answered hurriedly and gave the man the extra shillings he had promised him. He quckly walked in the direction of the docks. Here and there a lantern gleamed, the light shook, and a red glare flickered from an outward-bound coal steamer. The slimy pavement looked eerie and dangerous.

Dorian Gray hurried toward the left, glancing back now and then to see if he was being followed. In about seven or eight minutes, he reached the small, shabby place that housed the opium den. He stopped and gave the secret knock that admitted him.

In one corner, a sailer sprawled over a table. At the bar, two tawdry women were drinking. At the far end of the room there was a little staircase, leading to a darkened, musty chamber. As Dorian hurried up its three steps, the heavy odor of opium met him. He heaved a deep breath, and his nostrils quivered with

A Small Shabby Place

anticipation.

When Dorian entered, a young man with blond hair, who was bending over a lamp lighting a long thin pipe, looked up at him and nodded. He was thin, wasted, with a look of doom about him.

"I didn't realize you would be here, Adrian," muttered Dorian.

"Where else would I be?" he answered listlessly. "None of my friends will speak to me now."

"I thought you had left England," said Dorian.

"Darlington is not going to do anything. My brother paid the bill at last. I don't care about anything any more," Adrian sighed. "As long as I have opium, I don't need any friends."

Dorian Gray winced and looked at the other people on the floor. They were laying on the ragged mattresses in grotesque, strange, positions. The twisted limbs, the gaping mouths, the staring eyes, made them look like crea-

A Look of Doom

tures from another world.

But Dorian knew what they felt. And what had driven them to this terrible place to escape their own thoughts and deeds!

Memory was eating away at him. He kept seeing the eyes of Basil Hallward looking at him. He needed opium to forget, yet something bothered him. The presence of Adrian Singleton in the corner, a man Basil had accused him of destroying, troubled him. He wanted to be where no one knew who he was. He wanted to escape from himself.

Not wanting to stay, Dorian turned around and walked to the door with a look of pain on his face.

A hideous laugh broke from the painted lips of one of the women. "Prince Charming! Are you leaving us?" she cackled as he departed.

"Curse you!" he answered. "Don't call me that."

She snapped her fingers. "Prince Charming is what you used to like to be called, ain't it?"

"Prince Charming!"

she yelled after him in a high-pierced shriek.

The drowsy sailor leaped to his feet as she spoke and looked around wildly. He rushed out in hot pursuit. Dorian Gray hurried along the quay through the drizzling rain. He wondered if the ruin of Singleton's life was his fault, as Basil had said. What did Adrian matter to him? His life, his ruin, was none of Dorian's concern.

Callous and concentrated on evil, Dorian quickened his pace, hoping to enter another opium den. He darted into a dim archway, a short cut to the degrading place, when suddenly he was seized from behind. Before he had time to defend himself, he was thrust against the wall with a brutal hand around his throat.

In a second, he heard the click of a revolver, saw the gleam of a gun pointed straight at his head, and the dusky form of a short, muscular man facing him.

"What do you want?" Dorian gasped. "What have I done to you?"

A Brutal Hand

"Keep quiet," said the man. "If you move, I'll shoot you. You wrecked the life of Sibyl Vane, my sister," he charged. "She killed herself and you are responsible for her death.

"I swore I would kill you in return. I had no clue, no trace. I knew only your pet name— Prince Charming. I heard it tonight. Make your peace with God, for you are about to die!"

Dorian grew sick with fear. "I never knew her," he pleaded. "I never heard of her. You are mad."

"You had better confess your sin, for as sure as I am James Vane, you are going to die. "Down on your knees," he commanded.

"I give you one minute to make your peace— no more. I board a ship for India tonight and I must do this first."

Dorian was paralyzed with terror. He did not know what to say or do when suddenly, a wild hope flashed across his brain.

"Stop!" Dorian cried. "How long ago did your sister die? Quick, tell me!"

"I Am James Vane."

"Eighteen years," replied James Vane. "Why do you ask me? What do the years matter?"

"Eighteen years," laughed Dorian, with a touch of triumph in his voice. "See me under the light and look closely at my face!"

James Vane hesitated. Then he seized Dorian and dragged him into the light. As dim as the wind-blown lantern was, it showed him the error he was about to make. This man could not be more than twenty. He had all the bloom of boyhood. Indeed, he seemed hardly older than his sister had been at the time of her death. He was not the man who had destroyed his sister's life. James Vane felt he had almost killed the wrong person! He loosened his hold on Dorian Gray and reeled back.

"My God!" he cried. "I almost murdered you! Forgive me, a chance word in that damned opium den set me on the wrong track."

He released Dorian, who hurried away. James Vane stood on the pavement in horror. After a little while, a black shadow crept out.

Loosening His Hold

"Why didn't you kill him?" hissed the decrepit woman who had been at the bar. "I knew you were following him when you rushed out. You should have killed him. He has lots of money and is as bad as bad can be."

"I want no man's money. I want a man's life. He's not the man I'm looking for. My man would be nearly forty by now. That one is little more than a boy."

The woman gave a bitter laugh. "A boy! Why, it's eighteen years since Prince Charming made me what I am. They say he sold himself to the devil for a pretty face. He hasn't changed in eighteen years," she added with a sickly leer.

"You lie!" cried James Vane.

She raised her hand up to heaven. "Before God, I am telling the truth! He is the worst one who comes here!"

James Vane rushed into the street to find Dorian Gray, but he was gone. When he looked back, the woman had also vanished.

"Prince Charming Made Me What I Am."

A Lavish Dinner Party

Chapter 18

A Second Murder

A week later Dorian Gray was sitting in the conservatory of Selby Royal, his country house, talking to the pretty Duchess of Monmouth who, with her husband, a weary-looking man of sixty, were among his twelve guests. Relieved he had eluded the violent James Vane, he held a lavish dinner party on his estate. There was a wild recklessness in his manner.

He was entertaining his friends with clever stories when he caught a face pressed against the window. He began to tremble as he caught his breath. James Vane was there, and watching him!

The next day he did not leave the house. He spent most of the time in his room, sick with the fear of dying. The sense of being hunted and tracked down began to dominate him.

Whenever he closed his eyes, he could see the sailor's angry face peering at him through the misty glass. But perhaps he had been only dreaming. Sibyl Vane's brother had not come back to kill him. He had sailed away on a ship to India. And, after all, the man did not know who he was. The mask of youth had saved him.

Even if it had been an illusion, how terrible to be haunted by ghosts! What sort of life would he have, always tortured by his past crimes? Why had he killed Basil? Why had he given in to that moment of madness? He relived the murder over and over—and saw each hideous detail of his crime.

Finally, he calmed down. He convinced himself that he had been the victim of an over-ac-

Watching Him!

tive imagination. After three days of staying in his house, imprisoned by his fears, he organized a hunting party for his guests and ventured out to the pine woods.

The freshly scented air that winter morning seem to bring him back to life. After breakfast, he walked with the duchess for an hour in the garden and then rode his horse across the park to join the shooting party.

He joined Sir Geoffrey, who was aiming his rifle at a rabbit in the distance. He fired and there were two cries heard. One, the cry of an animal in pain—the second, of a man in agony.

"Good heavens!" exclaimed Sir Geoffrey. "I hit a man!"

In a few moments, the groundsmen dragged a body away. Dorian turned in horror. It seemed that misfortune followed wherever he went. The murdered man had caught the full charge of the shot in his chest and had died instantly. No one knew who he was. They guessed that, since he had tattoos on both

"I Hit a Man!"

arms, he might be a sailor. Later, on hearing this news, Dorian jumped to his feet. He felt as if his heart had suddenly stopped beating. A terrible hope fluttered in him. "Did you saw a sailor? Is there anything that would tell us his name? Where is the body? I must see it at once."

"It's in an empty stable at the Home Farm, sir," answered one of his men. "The local people don't like to have that sort of thing in their houses. They say a corpse brings bad luck."

Dorian decided to go to the stables himself. He leaped onto a horse and raced towards the farm, galloping down the long avenue as hard as he could. The trees swept past him and wild shadows flung themselves across his path. The stones flew from beneath his horse's feet. At last he reached the Home Farm. He dismounted and hurried to the stable door. There he paused for a moment, feeling he was on the brink of an important discovery, a discovery that would either make or destroy his life.

Leaping Onto a Horse

On a heap of sacking lay the dead body of a man in a coarse shirt and blue trousers. A spotted handkerchief had been placed over his face. A candle, stuck in a bottle, dripped slowly beside it.

Dorian shuddered. But he steeled himself and removed the cloth from the battered face. The man who had been shot in the woods was James Vane! He stood there for some minutes, looking at the dead body.

As he rode home, Dorian felt an enormous weight lift. He was safe at last.

James Vane

"I Want to be Better."

Chapter 19

Confronting Sin

"It's no good telling me that you are going to be good," grinned Lord Henry at Dorian, as he treated himself to caviar. "You are quite perfect. I hope you never change."

Dorian Gray shook his blond head and ran a tired hand through his hair. "No, I have done too many dreadful things in my life. I refuse to do any more. From now on, I vow to be good. You are so busy mocking everything, Harry. You do not realize the importance of goodness. I want to be better. I am going to be better."

Then he waved his hand in a casual manner

as he sat down. "Enough about me. Tell me about yourself. What's going on in town? I have not been to my club in days," he said, frowning slightly and pouring himself some wine.

"People are still talking about Basil's strange disappearance," reported Lord Henry. "The British public loves to gossip. You'd think my divorce and poor Alan Campbell's suicide would be enough to occupy them. Instead, they are captivated by the mysterious disappearance of an artist. Scotland Yard is on the case. The British police insist that the man in the gray suit who left for Paris on the midnight train was Basil. The French police claim Basil never arrived in Paris at all."

Dorian said nothing, but rose from the table and sat down at the piano. He let his fingers stray across the black and white keys. He sat quietly with his thoughts before he spoke.

"Did it ever occur to you that Basil Hallward might have been murdered?" asked Dorian.

At the Piano

"Basil was very popular and had no enemies. Why would anyone kill him?" Lord Henry wondered.

"I was very fond of Basil," Dorian said with a trace of sadness in his voice. "But I've heard people say he was murdered."

"Oh, some of the newspapers do. It does not seem at all likely to me. I know there are dangerous places in Paris, but Basil wasn't the sort of man to go to them," said Lord Henry. "Basil was very dull and he had lost his genius for painting. He probably fell off a bus in Paris."

"What if I told you, Harry, that I killed Basil?" asked Dorian slyly. He watched the older man intently after he had spoken. But Lord Henry did not seem shocked.

"I would say you were lying. Dorian, it is not in you to commit a murder. Crime is vulgar and you are not a vulgar man. It belongs to the lower classes. Anyway, murder is always a mistake. You should not do things you can't

"Crime is Vulgar."

talk about after dinner," Lord Henry laughed.

Dorian heaved a sigh and Lord Henry strolled across the room and began to stroke the head of a Java parrot, a large gray-feathered bird with a pink crest and a tail, balancing on a bamboo perch.

"Yes," he sighed, "Basil's paintings had been quite awful these last few years. When you and he stopped being friends, he stopped being a great artist. I think you inspired him. And artists can't afford to lose their inspiration."

Then Lord Henry wondered aloud about what happened to the portrait that Basil had painted of Dorian all those years ago. "You know," he said, "I've always loved that painting. It was Basil's best work. It captured your youth. I remember you told me it had been sent down to Selby Royal and somehow lost. What a pity! It was really a masterpiece."

Dorian shook his head. "I never really liked it. The memory of the thing is hateful to me."

"And yet, though it's been 20 years since you

"What Happened to the Portrait?"

sat for the painting, you haven't changed a bit. Play me a Chopin sonata on the piano and tell me, Dorian, how do you manage to keep your good looks? You must have a secret. I am only ten years older than you and I am wrinkled and worn." Lord Henry sighed.

"You, on the other hand, look great," he added. "Indeed, you look exactly the same as you did on the day we met. The tragedy of old age is not that one is old, but that one is young. What a wonderful life you have had, Dorian."

"I am not the same," Dorian insisted.

But his words fell on deaf ears. Lord Henry refused to listen. He recounted all the beauty and passion, the perfection and good fortune of his friend's life. He said that he wished he could change places with him. He claimed that life had been good to Dorian. He said that life was Dorian Gray's art, the art of living well.

"Yes, life has been good. But I'm not going to have the same life any more," Dorian said, rising from the piano. "Stop saying these ridicu-

"I Am Wrinkled and Worn."

lous things. You don't know me at all! I think that if you did, even you would turn away from me!"

Lord Henry was stunned by Dorian's words. He switched subjects, chatting casually of clothes and parties. Then he looked at Dorian and said, "You cannot change to me. You and I will always be friends."

Dorian's eyes narrowed as he spoke. "Yet you poisoned me with a book. I won't ever forgive you for that! Promise me that you won't give that book to anyone else. It does great harm."

But Lord Henry refused to listen. He was a self-centered man who could not stand criticism. "Don't moralize, Dorian. You sound like a parent warning his children against sin. Instead," he invited, "meet me tomorrow. Lady Branksome wants to discuss buying some paintings." Lord Henry thought Dorian could help her chose wisely.

Dorian reluctantly agreed to meet them and Lord Henry left.

"You Poisoned Me with a Book."

Restless and Agitated

Chapter 20

A Bitter End

The following day was so warm that Dorian strolled through the park on his way home from the Branksomes' townhouse. He saw several people point him out and whisper to each other. In the past, he would have been flattered by the attention; now he was just tired.

He arrived home and found his servant waiting up for him. He sent him to bed and threw himself on the sofa in the library. Dorian felt restless and agitated. He could not stop thinking about some of the things that Lord Henry had said to him.

He wondered: Was it really true that one could never change? He suddenly felt a yearning for his lost boyhood—a time when he had been truly good. He knew that he had long since corrupted himself and that he had exerted an evil influence on others.

What was worse, Dorian thought, he had enjoyed ruining other people's lives. He had taken special pleasure in disgracing those who were most full of promise. But was *his* life forever ruined? Was there no hope? What was responsible for his terrible ways? He blamed Lord Henry's evil book and Basil's portrait for everything.

Now he knew what a monstrous thing he had wished for in eternal youth and beauty. Why had he said those fateful words? If he hadn't prayed for his wish to be answered, he might have led a better life. All his failure had been due to this. He hated his good looks—and his youth. But for those two things, his life might have been truly happy. Instead, beauty

Was There No Hope?

had mocked him, and youth had spoiled him.

Dorian was finally confronting his own life—and he did not like what he saw. Sibyl Vane had poisoned herself when he treated her cruelly. Her brother, James Vane, was hidden in a nameless grave in the country. Alan Campbell had shot himself one night in his laboratory, but hadn't revealed Dorian's secret that he had been forced to keep. Dorian had escaped being associated with all three of their deaths. Even the death of Basil Hallward had passed from public interest. He was safe there, too.

What weighed upon Dorian Gray's mind wasn't the suicides or the murders, but the living death of his own soul!

All I want, prayed Dorian, is a new life! He would never again tempt innocence. He would be fine and upstanding. Perhaps his decision to be good could change the ugly face in the painting. He would go and look. He took a lamp from the table and crept upstairs. Yes, he would be good and the painting would no

Alan Campbell Had Shot Himself.

longer terrify him. He felt as though a load had been lifted from him.

As he unlocked the door, he dragged the purple covering from the portrait. A cry of pain and indignation broke from his lips. He could not see any change. The thing was still hateful—even more than before! The eyes had a look of deep cunning and the mouth was curved in a malicious sneer.

The scarlet dew that had spotted the hand after Basil's murder seemed brighter, and more like new blood! Was the red stain larger than before? It seemed to have crept like a horrible disease over the wrinkled fingers. There was even blood at the feet—as though the thing had dripped—and even on the hand that had not held the knife!

What did it all mean? Did the painting want him to confess his many sins? The idea was insane! What if he did? The world would laugh, Dorian decided. There was no trace of his guilt anywhere. He had gotten away with every one

Like a Horrible Disease!

of his crimes.

And if he told people the story of how the painting kept changing, they would call him crazy and lock him up in an institution. And if he showed it to them, who would believe such an outrageous tale? But Basil's murder—was it to dog him all his life? Was he ready to confess? Never!

Dorian made a fateful decision. He refused to be burdened by his past, ever. There was only one piece of evidence against him: The painting. He would destroy it. He had only kept it because it had given him pleasure to watch it grow old. Lately, he felt no such pleasure.

The blasted painting had kept him up at night. When he was away, he had been terrified that someone else might see it. The painting had brought sadness to his passions. Its very existence had destroyed moments of joy and happiness. It had been like a bad conscience to him. He would destroy that conscience and start fresh.

He Would Destroy It.

Dorian look around and saw the knife that had stabbed Basil Hallward. He had cleaned it many times, until there was no stain left on it. It was bright and it glistened. As it had killed the painter, so it would also kill the painter's work and all that it represented. It would kill the past and when that was dead, Dorian Gray would be free. He would kill this painted monster and he would be set free.

He seized the knife and stabbed the picture with it.

There was a terrible cry—and a crash. The cry was so horrible that the frightened servants ran upstairs. Two gentlemen who were passing in the square below stopped and looked up at the great house.

They ran to get a policeman and brought him back. They rang the bell several times, but there was no answer. Except for a light in one of the top windows, the house was all dark.

Inside, the servants were talking to each other in low whispers. The old housekeeper